Days Beside Ourselves

— Year 1 —

Real People | Real Love | Real Poetry

Warren Christopher Taylor

For you

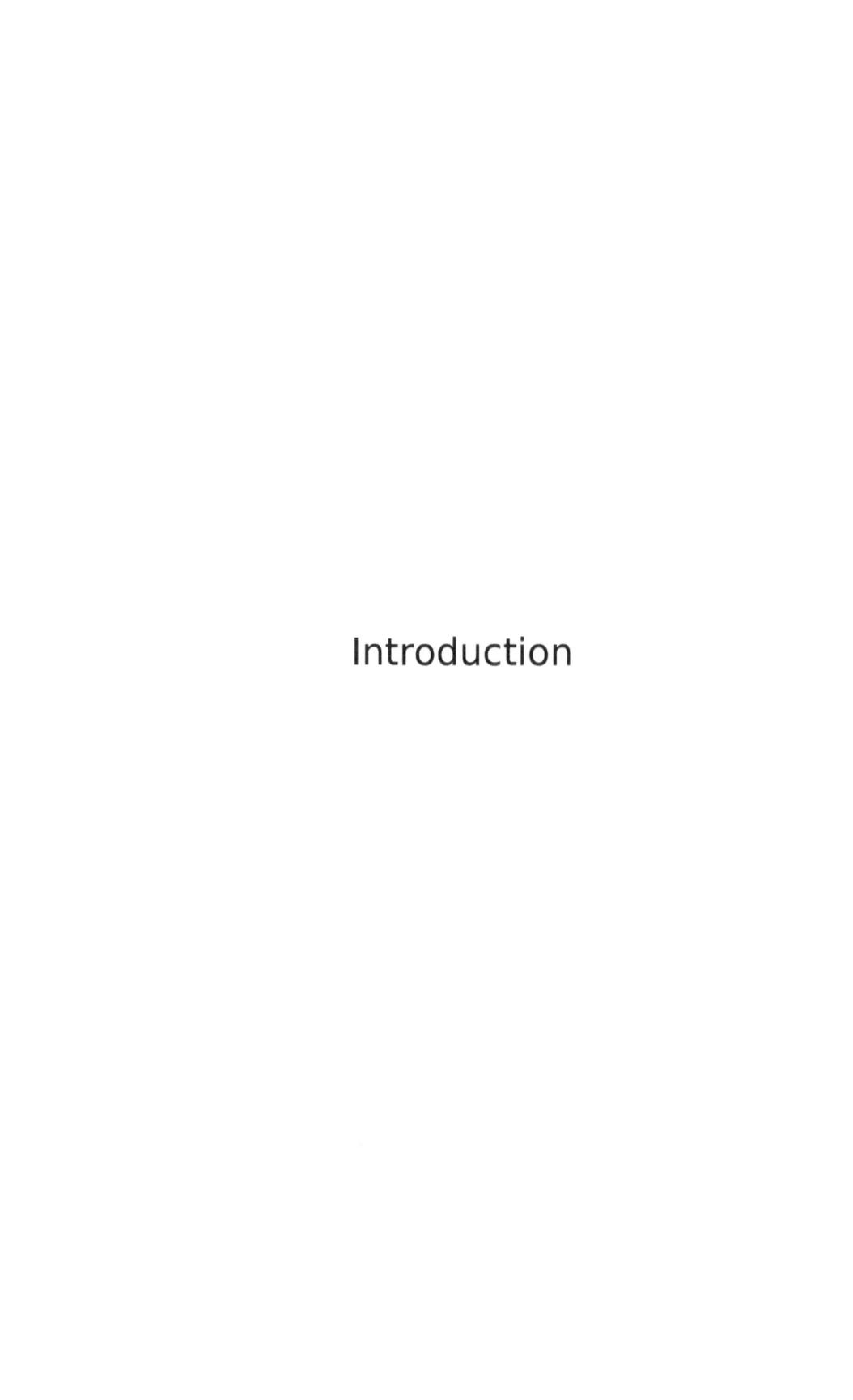

Introduction

Meeting: Their Introduction

As raindrops pour, we wake beside ourselves
And no one else. We fill our morning drone
With silent breakfast, endless empty shelves
Of social, rainy walks to work alone

Until we turn a corner bumping one
Another. Dropping everything we hold,
The earth continues rolling round the sun;
But both our constant heartbeat throbs stop cold

Along with breathing uncontrolled. We can't
Hold back our stares from one another's eyes.
Despite our tries to catch our breaths, we pant
Then catch ourselves and break from our surprise.

We bend to get our things. The sun expands.
But, as we bend, we touch each other's hands.

Courtship

Sighing, Staring, Waiting

Staring at our phones with these thoughts of "Come on!
Write a message! Call!" while we try to act cool -
Failing as we make ourselves' wait so long drawn
"Well," we both mutter,

"Guess I'll have to focus on something else. You'll
Call at some point, maybe." But waiting feels so
Full of sighing, staring at nothing. "How cruel,"
Both of us mumble,

"Thought we had a moment." We guess not. Hearts go
Sinking in our chests as the sun sets our hope.
"Can't hold on forever," we tell ourselves. So,
Typing aflutter,

Both of us text out, "Hey," while our wishes wild grope,
Heartbeats in our throats, as our phones' rings help cope.

Overlook

She leans against a tree and says, "You know
This might not be the way." While laughing, "Two
More minutes, then you'll see," he says. A glow
Of sunlight glints between the leaves. "The view

Is really sweet," he smiles and leads the way.
She takes a breath and groans. She rolls her eyes
And wipes a bead of sweat that starts to stray
Around her cheek. The path ahead, she sighs,

Appears to never end. "We're almost there!"
He yells. But underneath her breath she moans,
"Like I can tell." She gripes, "This guy... I swear."
He grins, "We're here," as birds chirp singing tones.

She sighs and laughs as midday sunlight beams A
mountain's valley carved by river streams.

Secret Oasis

"It's late," he says, "You sure it's open still?"
"Of course," she smiles and leads him holding hands
Down maze-like streets - the autumn moonlight chill.
His look could kill. He sighs and doubts her plans.

But on they go down streets and alleyways
He knows the neighborhood but still can't place
Exactly where they are. Her thoughts in flames,
She rushes through the dark. The place she aims

For stands in lights against the city night -
A brilliant castle right beside the park.
She greets the guard, who smiles with such a spark,
And walks in like she owns the place. The sight

Of quite a forest in the courtyard, first
Just makes him gasp. She watches him with
thirst.

Nothing Happened. Right?

Above the skyline, rising red and blue,
Confused, alone inside his bedroom, "How?
We didn't do... So how did I...? I knew..."
Her eyes glare darts around his room, "And now

He isn't even here? The hell?" A swell
Of anger with disgrace, her thoughts feel drowned.
She shakes her head to put them down and tell
Herself "OK". She stands and hears a sound.

She sighs, "At least the view is nice." She goes
To tiptoe down the hall — unsurely creep —
And finds him, cook in kitchen like he knows
His way around. She glowers through her sleep.

He smiles, "You dozed off — shoulder laid your head."
(She scowls.) "So I just moved you to my bed."

Dressing Room

"That one's nice," he says. But she shakes her head. "No,"
Frowning with her face to the side, "The styles clash."
Shrugging, "Sure," he tells her, "It still looks class, though."
Sighing, she shucks off

All the clothes. He leans to observe, gets whiplash
Turning back so fast when she comes out new clad.
"Sexy. Mmm," he smiles. But she squints her eyelash,
"Fine, but not perfect."

Laughing, checking time on his phone, "Well, not bad
Might suffice to make it on time. She comes dressed,
Perfect in his eyes. In her own, she smiles glad.
"Dazzling," he tells her.

Turning round, she saunters so self-possessed,
Leaning down, they kiss so their lips are both blessed.

Rain Check Picnic

She sulks as sideways high-wind rainstorms fall.
Against their window, lovely plans discard.
This deluge leaves her fragile feelings scarred.
He shakes his head with wonder when a small
Impression calls. He smiles as thought flames sprawl
Inside him, "Great idea." Her wishes marred,
She asks him, "What?" her hopeful feelings charred.
He says, "Oh, nothing," rushing down the hall.

He picks a blanket from his closet rack,
Collects his plants from all the window rims,
And from his fridge he takes some food to snack.
She sighs as thunder rumbles lightning hymns.
He sets their picnic, starts a music track.
She turns in shock as her amusement brims.

Gourmet Longings

"So posh," she leans and whispers with a smile.
"Oh yeah?" he looks around, "I couldn't tell."
"Yeah, right," she laughs, "You have expensive style."
He makes the thinking face, "Let me dispel

This thought right now." She sways, "Dispel away."
"I know the chef," he claims, "On Saturday
We volunteer together." "Volunteer?"
He says, "We cook for homeless people near

The river." Pausing, she's confused, "You cook?"
"I do. I love to cook," he swears. She grins.
He says, "And this guy's cooking really wins."
She leers, "I like this guy." He gives the look.

She vows, "I like you more, though." "Sure you do,"
He scowls. She vies, "I'm really into you."

The Omelette Test

She glares and runs her fingers through her hair.
"Are you for real?" she asks. He tries to ease
His dire straits, "I mean… it's only fair.
Plus I'll be there. This omelette thing's a breeze."

She groans, "I'm not applying for a job."
He moans, "I know. I know. It's just to show
That we can bond together." Near a sob,
She stares afar. Between her lips, breaths blow.

She tries avoiding eyes and slow she stands
Without a glance at him. "All right," she calls,
"So what am I supposed to do?" He hands
Her eggs, a fork and bowl. His timbre falls,

"I think we'll be magnificent as one."
She gripes, "I guess we'll find out once we're done."

Interlude — I

Time: 01:23 AM
From: Him
Title: Shadow of Desire (What do you think?)

Once, life was days filled light with darkness.
Now, these days grow dim in view of you.
One thought of you and all else comes through
Dark. Try reading something; think of you.
The words bleed off the page and colour
All the world an inky hue, all dull
Except for you - who renders daylight
Dusk. In light of you, the sun's last rays
Retreat behind your constant shadow.

Firstcation

Holy S#!? Class

Final airplane seats at the back, before they
Sit, the flight attendant drifts over, "Hi there."
"Huh," they stand with luggage in hand. Her kind way,
"So," the attendant

Says, "two first-class passengers no-showed their fare."
"Oh? Is that right?" both of them ask. She smiles wide,
"Yes. And now we're offering you to both share."
"What the.." they stutter.

"Yes!" they say. She shows them the way to joy's side.
On the way, they pass the unfit, below par
People. At the door, the attendant turns stride,
Letting them into

Heaven. "Oh... my... goodness," their mouths and eyes jar.
Fortune shows them life as a brilliant bright star.

No Report Resort

She whispers, "Is this place a real resort?"
He starts, "I mean…" but never quite completes.
The palm trees coconut and seas transport;
But something's strange about the empty streets.

The staff all stare off downbeat far away.
Their maître 'd contorts his face to say,
"Your room is here," and leaves. She goes, "That's so…"
He stops, "He cared as far as he could throw."

She shakes her head, "You said you checked it out?"
He rubs his eyes, "I did. Reviews were fine."
She lays down on the bed and on her spine
She feels a poke and finds out what about.

"What's wrong?" he frowns. She shows some tool and waits.
She's shocked to see the shaft-shaped tool vibrates.

Fish Gone Fishing

They stand atop a pearl-white strip of sand
Arriving from the sea. The sailboat's mate
Who brought them starts a cooking flame by hand.
They watch, in awe, his first mate set a bait

And, in a flash, he has his prey. "Oh wow!"
She says. He nods his head, "That's crazy skill."
The other's flame and grill are ready now.
They watch the first mate bring to him his kill.

A swift strike fishing knife removes its head.
She winces, shocked. They rip off both the fins
"What's wrong?" he says. Her eyes are filled with dread.
The mates start cooking after scaling skins.

He sees a teardrop leaking from her eye.
She says, "I didn't know we'd watch it die."

Nightsnorkeling

There isn't any sound but rolling tide —
Not even wind through palm leaves. Moonlight bleeds
Across the night — a guide. The tide recedes.
They wade in knee deep first then slowly slide Between
the surface and the sea. Inside
Their masks they breathe. They switch on light that leads
Their spying on the deep. She quickly speeds
Ahead, amazed by all the life. Beside

Himself, he stirs to reach her. Blue and red
And yellow fish weed through the coral reef.
He gives her chase while all inside her head,
She can't contain her joyful disbelief.
The boundless ocean leaves his voice for dead.
She swims away from all his silent grief.

Study vs Knowledge

Weary, wandered far from their refuge, "Where... are
We?" she wonders. Scanning, he says, "Well...
Hmm. So I don't know." She stops as her legs feel like tar,
Tired from walking.

"Ask someone the way?" she suggests. His eyes grow
Narrow, searching, "Maybe, I guess." his words quake.
Shyly stopping someone, he mutters, voice low,
Fragmented babble.

When the other person can't make his words make
Sense, they walk off after they give up. Frown wide,
Hostile, "Thought you spoke it," she sighs, "For god's sake."
Staring obliquely,

"No," he says, "I **studied** it. Plus, I still tried."
"No, you said you spoke it" she says, "You still lied."

Innocent Caress

She winces, moaning slight. He says, "That's tight."
"This muscle needs some spotlight." "Yeah," she sighs —
His hands caress her outer thighs, dig right
Inside. She takes a deep breath, almost cries,

Out loud - but stops. Her nearly silent whine Attends
his stroking ointment down her spine.
"Right here?" he asks. "Mm hmm," she rolls beside
Herself with bliss inside. His fingers glide

Around her butt and walk across a wire
Between her legs for just a moment's time —
Before she comprehends his fatal crime.
She spirals in the sand, her eyes on fire.

She frowns until his smile sets her at ease.
She begs, "Don't go so deep in public, please."

Parting Paradise

Their luggage packed, they hold their hands. They stand
Outside their hideaway. That faraway
Refrain of ocean waves unfolds the day,
Their final daybreak rising from the sand.
Beside, their concierge insists demand
To wait along with them. They both betray
Annoyance, staring at the seabirds stray
Across the sky. Their fingers clutch their hand,

Impatient, yet averse to say, "Goodbye,"
They check the time yet turn their eyes to find
The sea before they join the birds up high.
Their taxi pulls up though they're both resigned
To take their seats inside. They deeply sigh
Their ride away with futile looks behind.

Interlude — II

Official Confessions

Our friends all ask, "You seeing that one still?"
We roll our eyes, laugh, "That one? Yes I am."
Their eyes grow wide. They lean in close, drawl, "Damn..."
Are you for real?" We feel a silent thrill.
Our friends all say, "My god!" soprano shrill.
They all ask questions in a rushing slam.
We shake our heads, "This feels like an exam."
"It is!" they say as one, "Come on now. Spill."

We both ignore and look to check our phone.
Our friends lean back among themselves and sneer.
We're each in crowded rooms but feel alone.
We text, "Let's catch a movie somewhere near?"
We answer "Sure." Our friends continued drone,
We leave, "Goodbye," before they see or hear.

Long Weekend

The Parents Call

"No," she tells her phone on her ear, "He's not dead."
Seconds pass. He watches across her front room.
"Why? I mean…" she wonders annoyed with deep dread,
"What would the point be?"

Shakes her head and throws up her hand, her eyes gloom.
"Right, all right, all right," she relents but still glares,
Waving him to come to her side. He's shocked - doom
Dragging across the

Room. He sits down flustered and shoots her "Huh?" stares.
Turning on the speaker, she rolls her eyes wide,
"Uh, hello?" he mumbles. Her mother's voice blares,
Something outlandish.

"Come on, mom," she breaks off, "we'll be there wide- eyed."
"What?" he gasps. She mumbles, "Goodbye," to mom's side.

Officially For Real

She runs her fingers through her hair and sighs
As sunlight glimmers far away
Escape the sky. He says, "That pilot flies
Just like they're drunk. It's such a crazy day."

She stares into the distance, straying home
When he asks, "Hey, are you okay?" A roam
Absorbed within her thoughts, she says, "I'm fine.
"I guess," she sighs, "it's time." They chart a line

To find their ride. She looks across the place
But doesn't find their face. She shakes her head.
He says, "I'm sure she's on her way." Instead,
Across the room, a woman's footsteps trace

Their way to them. At once, "Well, hey, I guess"
Her mother's voice strikes both of them with stress.

The Dead Mall

They walk in silence through some midday mall
Until she asks him, "Are you mad at me?"
He echoes, "Why exactly, first of all?"
Her parents wander browsing ten steps free.

She grieves, "It's bad your answer asked me back."
"It's just," he says, "This mall feels like a shack."
"A what?" she gapes. He says, "A shopping slum."
She grins and shakes her head, "That sounds so dumb."

"And yet so true," he smiles. She laughs out loud.
And asks, "So you're not mad about the trip?"
He stops, "If so, why wouldn't I just skip?"
She takes his hand and smiles as if she's proud.

He leans, "Your folks have vanished. They aren't there."
"Oh, they'll be fine," she turns, "They'll both take care."

Original Sequel

She says, "We really need to buy before we go."
Her parents shrug, "We can't just get them there?"
She throws her hands up with a baffled stare.
He deals, "Let's buy the tickets for the show,
While on our way." The parties let it go
And nod, reluctant - as they leave their lair.
Her father — buddy-buddy — "Hey, come share.
You liked the first one?" He says, "I don't know."

I never watched." Her dad says, "Who are you?"
"You never saw the best film ever made?"
He sees her laughing and her mother too.
He tells him, "No, I didn't." unafraid.
She tells them, "All right, we've got things to do."
Her father gives the side-eye, throwing shade.

Storms of Fireworks

His head shakes, eyes roll. "Whoa!" she turns around.
He stops behind them, lost among the crowd.
She sees him stiffen up and hit the ground.
Her mind blank, mouth unclosed, the night a shroud,

Her mom's words blurred, "Let's turn him on his side."
 She sees his body jerking in the grass,
The sounds don't reach her ears before they've died.
Each sand grain slows down through her hourglass.

Below, there's only darkness in his head.
A tiny offshoot crowd of watchers forms
To wonder whether he's alive or dead.
She sees him slowly come to just as storms

Of fireworks begin to fill the sky
His eyes reflect as she begins to cry.

Farewell Omen

Lined to board, no speaking between them. Not sure
Where to go from here with their thoughts in surplus.
Near them, other passengers trek on their pure
Trouble- free travels.

They avoid their eyes so they never discuss
Any aspect. Still, in the air, it breathes through
Goading them to dwell on it till they concuss.
"Boarding of zone one,"

Echoes on the speakers. She asks him, "Have you
Seen someone about it?" He says, "Well, sort of.
I'll make more appointments." She holds his hand new
— Boarding together

Like some kind of blessing from high up above
Their eternal struggle to deepen their love.

Interlude — III

The One? Two? Three?

"Vacation, huh?" our friends lean in, "Report."
We roll our eyes but shyly smile, "On what?"
"We left. We came back." "What the what?" they snort,
"Give details." "Facts?" we ask. They sing, "Uncut.

"The whole truth." "Sure," we turn our eyes askew
And spew some stories made up off the shoot.
Our smiles both fraught to see our friends all chew
Them up with glee. Our eyes turn up to loot

More lies from in the trees. We scan the sky
Across the city. Neither of us finds
What more to say. We let the moment by.
Our friends sit widened eyes, exploded minds,

They ask, "The one?" — like pulling out a rug.
We close our eyes and wonder, turn and shrug.

The Big Step

Question Time

Relaxing on her sofa half-undressed,
Her head laid on his chest, he stands to go Get
something — more familiar than a guest.
She leans to watch him walk like it's a show

And even presses pause on what was on,
So much he turns back, his attention drawn.
He smiles and asks, "You liking what you see?"
She smirks, "I guess it looks all right to me."

He brings a cup, "Your lease is over soon?"
Surprise in verses drafted on her face,
She asks, "And if it is, then what's the case?"
He softly strokes her cheek beneath the moon,

"My lease ends too. I think we both can guess."
She smiles, "I guess our thing is a success."

New Flat Spreadsheet

She writes, "So check these out. They're all quite chic."
He clicks the link but sees that it's a file
Whose download starts and takes a good long while.
He thinks out loud, "That seems a bit... unique."
She writes again, "I used a cool technique.
I hope you like it." "Huh?" he mulls awhile.
He shakes his head and sends a thinking smile
Emoji, but no other words to speak.

He finds a spreadsheet in the loaded link
And looks on wide-eyed, shocked at how complete
She's been. He writes, "I really didn't think
You'd make a spreadsheet. This is really... neat."
She sends a kissing face emoji wink,
"I'm glad you like it. It was quite a feat."

Tour

They say in one voice, "Ooh! That view is great!"
Their chaperone says, "Sure, I guess it's fine,"
And makes an aural sigh. She hears the hate
Beneath their voice and whispers, "Out of line."

He calms, "It's cool. They won't be on the lease."
She shakes her head and checks the closet space
By stepping in. She feels her grief increase
And frowns her whole entire face, "This place

Is not like what we saw online. Like how
Is this a walk-in?" "Hmm," their guide just shrugs.
She takes his hand and says, "We're leaving now."
He tells their guide, "Well, thanks - I guess," and lugs

Behind. He says, "I liked the place we viewed."
She snaps, "I won't live where the staff are rude."

Trust No Condo

"Really sexy lobby," he whispers. "Hmm. Sure.
Doorman wasn't there," she complains. Their guide
Wears a smile, their hand out to shake, "I hope you're
Ready for awesome."

"Right," she glares. He chuckles perturbed and, tongue- tied,
"Hey, there. Hi," A welcoming smile, their guide takes
Everything in stride, "Well, I guess the lift ride
Maybe should win you —

Comfort, style and quick." So they fly up; two shakes
Home in a jiff. Easing, she grunts with, "That's fair."
"Progress," smiles their guide. And they both have heart quakes
Views to the outside.

"Now to see the closets," she slides her way there —
Smiling as she enters with space she could spare.

The Educated Guess

He droops back in his chair and checks his phone
Up in the air. He takes a latte sip.
She sits and wears her face so in the zone,
It makes him slip. The lunch crowd makes their trip.

She takes a notebook out, her laptop too,
Three writing pens and sticky notes brand new.
He thinks out loud, "The hell?" She says, "Prepared.
I come prepared." He looks a little scared

But shakes his head and asks, "So where to move?"
She squints, "My data tells me... I don't know."
He laughs and rubs his eyes, "OK, let's throw
The data out. Which place just hits that groove?"

She droops back, looks up at the ceiling, "Well..."
He smiles. She shoots, "By now then you can tell."

Move In Day

He brings their last box up. She brings a lamp.
They shut their new apartment door and slack
Beside their window view. His fingers clamp
Around her hand. She holds his hand right back.

He leaves the light a little while to find
A box with things they need. The window's blind
Breaks sunlight into streams. Behind, she hears
Him move some things and then a crash. Her fears

Come on her fast. She rushes over past
Their stacks of boxes, "Oh, my god." He's out
And seizing on the floor. She turns about
His body on his side. His spasms last

But minimize. They sit in beams of sun
That gleam around the two of them as one.

Interlude — IV

That One Friend

Our friends all shake their heads as we replay.
They go, "You got the ring? A wedding date?"
We roll our eyes, "Calm down. Right now it's great."
They laugh, "Oh really, now? We'll see," they say.
We sigh a bit inside and scoff, "OK."
They go on, "Tell." Our stories escalate
And leave them in a captivated state.
That one friend asks us, cutting off halfway,

"It all sounds too... fantastic. What's the catch?"
We shrug our shoulders, slant our heads, "We're good."
That 'friend', "How you before I've found a match?"
"Just luck," we glare as dirty as we could
And think what bitter vengeance we can hatch.
They hush and blush exactly like they should.

Fears & Superstitions

There Was a Ghost

"There **was** a ghost," she says. "It wasn't my
Imagination." "No, of course. I know,"
He says and holds her close. She says, "So why Don't
you believe me, then?" He laughs, "I so

Believe you, love. I do." And she laughs too
But stops to yawn and say, "You don't. But wait,
And soon you'll find a ghost is haunting you,
And then you'll run to me." "I will?" "Your fate

Will be in my hands." "Isn't it in yours
Already?" "Baby, please don't interrupt."
He strokes her hair in silence. "All our doors
Will open..." but a yawn and sleep disrupt

Her omen as she sinks in his embrace.
He leaves a forehead kiss to save her place.

Knife Work Worry

"Not quite," he frowns, "Just make a smoother pass."
She shakes her head, "How all these years I've had
"To cook before we met?" With sigh and sass,
She rolls her eyes, "You really drive me mad."

"Let's go. Come learn the proper way to cut."
She turns to him and holds her hips and butt.
He motions, "Here," and takes the knife by stem
She backs off even though her eyes condemn.

A deep breath, "First," he motions with his eyes,
"Like so," and curls his hand up like a claw.
He looks up, eyes a question. "Yeah, I saw,"
She shoots back. Fast he cuts until he cries

Surprised his middle finger's bloody red.
She smiles but helps him clean the blood he's shed.

Whistling In Debt

Chopping up tomatoes to eat with fried eggs;
Playing music, swaying his head with headphones;
Whistling while he works; from the bedroom, she begs
"Baby! The whistling!"

Bright and blithe, he scrambles the eggs. Her loud groans
Echo down the hallway. She says, "Just please quit
"Whistling!" Then she sees he has headphones on — moans.
Dancing a bit, he

Turns around to see her, and smiles. Her frostbit
Frown replies. She pulls off his headphones, "Stop this
Whistling!" "Why?" he asks with a grin. A soft hit
Sore on his shoulder,

"Whistling loses money!" her words all but hiss.
Eyes rolled, "Sure," he leaves on her cheek a soft kiss.

Metro Cabin Fever

She grips the railing, breathes in deep and sighs —
The full-up metro flying down the track.
Her heartbeat racing, breathing short, she tries
To keep composed. But hot against her back

She feels the riders' gazes bearing down,
The subway swerving, jolting underground.
Abruptly, like a bolt, it's like the town
And all its people altogether pound

Against her chest at once until she soon
Feels breathless, senses vanished from her head.
She nearly faints from underneath a swoon
That wilts her legs. He watches, filled with dread,

Her vacant body sinking down the wall
But holds her close before her looming fall.

Stray

Out of that Italian café, they walk back
Home fulfilled, with traffic exhausted, moonlight
Bright, and time to kill. As a vagrant jet black
Cat on its tiptoes

Meets them at the crosswalk, she stops their tracks right
There. He asks, "What's wrong?" With her hand on heart, "Wait.
We should walk a different…" turned backward, hand tight
 Grabbing his arm to

Run away, she hurries them off. He smiles, "Great.
Scared of cats now?" Turning, she checks. That black cat
Stalks behind them. Shocked, with her racing heart rate,
"Hurry!" she hollers.

"Huh?" he wonders. Rushing, she breaks to run flat
Out - with him a daze - to escape that black cat.

A Sneeze For You

She covers up her mouth and nose, "Ahchoo!"
Recoiling fast and loose. He pays no mind,
Just read his texts aloof. She scowls, "How kind
"Of you." He looks up, "What?" She glares askew,
"Ahchoo!" again. He rolls his eyes, "You blew
"Your brains out almost there." She says, "You'd find
"A way to carry on, I'm sure." Resigned
To read some more, he turns as though they're through.

She rolls her eyes and says, "I could have used
"A blessing there from you." He wonders, "Why?"
And turns his face up, looking all bemused.
"It's just polite," she says, "since I could die."
"Yeah, right," he smiles, "from sneezing." Unamused,
She sneezes in his face and says, "You try."

Ladder to Hell

He throws his hands up, "Take the whole damn path
"Of course." She rubs his lower back, replies,
"Just walk around." He tries. Asks, "Where?" with wrath
At them, not her. She hems and haws and sighs

He says, "You see?" and takes off underneath
The ladder. But she frowns and grits her teeth,
"No, wait! Not there! Let's walk a different way."
Confused, he stares a skeptical display,

"The place is only three doors down the street."
She stammers, stutters, "We can't walk down
here Beneath this evil ladder," filled with fear.
He shakes his head, relinquished in retreat

"Whatever. Sure," he says. She smiles and takes
The long way round in case the ladder breaks.

One Flew at the Windowpane

She folds up all her delicates then eyes
His underwear, uncertain. "No," she shakes
Her head and starts to call his name but spies
A bird behind the windowpane. It takes

A step across the ledge and pecks the glass.
She gasps and drops her clothes, unfolding, "No."
She shakes her head and yells his name. A mass
Of silence passes by. She tells it, "Go!"

She glares. The bird glares back. It pecks once more
And flies away. He comes and asks, "What's wrong?"
"That bird!" she points. He stands just in the door
And leans, "What bird?" She turns, groans, "Ugh…" so long

She doesn't see the bird return in flight
And slam into their window out of spite.

The Return of Black Cat

She hears him coming in the house. He hears
Her in the shower, leaves the door ajar —
Forgetting — let's that cat slip in. She clears
The mirror with her hand. He clears the bar
And island for the bags. That cat walks through
Their house unseen. She calls, "You got the eggs?"
He frowns, says, "Uhh…" and lets it miss its cue.
She shakes her head and dries her breasts and legs.
She hears the bathroom door and looks that way
But only sees the hallway; starts to speak
But screams instead. The black cat's furry fray
Has brushed her leg. He rushes in, a streak,
"What's wrong?" She says, "That black cat!" "Where?"
He looks but stops to watch her standing there.

Miserable Mirror

"Hmm," she checks the mirror for cracks or small flaws.
"Well?" he wonders, "Where are the blots you've spent
all "Day investigating to find?" Her clenched jaws,
Rolling her eyes, she

Grinds her teeth and sighs, "If I find them, I'll call."
"I'll just wait," he smiles, "by your side." she laughs, tense,
"Please don't sneer at me." As he comes and stands tall
Over her shoulder,

Fingers on her midriff, he makes her just wince —
Barely anything to discern. Except here,
In a flash, the mirror descends so fast, since
Letting it go, she

Reaches out to try and corral it. Great fear
Shatters like the mirror as both her eyes tear.

The Money Itch

She clears her throat and smiles a bit. The show
Goes on the screen. She can't stop scratching hands
And curls her lips up, frowning. "Let me know
"What's wrong," he says. She stops the show and stands

Up straight. She says, "My hand is itching." "Ooh,"
He laughs, "So, scratch it, then." "But, no. I mean
"My right palm itches." "Well, in that case, do
It more." She groans. He starts the show again. The scene

Continues on the screen. She shakes her head
And rolls her eyes. He laughs a bit and sighs
At something vaguely funny. Then, instead
Of going on, he stops the show and pries

Out words, annoyed, "My left palm itches." "Right,"
She smiles and pulls his arms around her tight.

Across Her Heart

She stretches out to touch across the bed
To feel his face and head so as to make
For certain he's still there. For once awake,
She rolls asleep - now made for sure her dread
Has faded. Still again he's in her head,
To spite it all. She feels a pall, an ache
Across her heart. Far off, she sees him take
Another woman's hand. A strand, a thread, a shred
Of gloom expands that she can barely stand.
She wonders where he found her in this vast
Expanse. She sees him falling for her charms —
Her horror. Slouched towards the holy land —
Grown distant in the shade their shadows cast —
They fade as she awakens in his arms.

The Thirteenth Return

They smile delighted - eyes as bright as stars — And
sparkle through the lobby into dark.
A block gone by beneath the sky, he bars
Their way, "I think I left my phone." Her stark

Expression - star collapsing - says it all.
He offers, all the same, "It's fine," a small Dismissive
wave and right back he returns.
She stops him, "No, you can't go back," she spurns

His journey. "What?" he wonders - palms up - "Why?"
She's silent. "Wow," he laughs and walks right past.
She groans and glares and follows after fast.
She calls behind him, "Baby, please just try

To trust me." But he keeps on through the door
And up the lift to reach the thirteenth floor.

She paces round the lobby. While in place
Up on the rooftop bar, he starts to say
He lost his phone. The maître 'd, with grace,
Just hands it over in a rare display,

"You have a nice day, sir." He smiles and takes
It, nods his "Thanks," and turns to go. He makes
The vacant elevator down before
The doors can slight him. "Nice," he taps his floor,

The lights shut off. The lift abruptly drops
Too fast then stops and throws him. "What the hell?"

He wonders. Down it speeds again - a swell
Of fear inside the dark - before it stops

A spark. His heartbeat with his breaths collide
While through the opened doors she waits outside.

Chilopodophobia

She wraps her body in his quilted
Embrace as music shuffles while
He strokes her hair. Her eyes have jilted
And chased away the day's last trial.

She hears his soothing voice is reading
Above the raindrops ceaseless pleading
Against the window. But she sees
It crawling, there. At once, she frees

Her eyes from sleeping, screams out, "Kill it!"
And leaps up on the sofa, "There!
"The centipede!" He wonders, "Where?"
Confused. "It's there!" she yells out, "Kill it!"

He laughs and finds it crawling. Fast
Beneath his shoe, it's dead at last.

Interlude — V

Perhaps as clouds and rain ordain the fall,
My love for you floods through me;
Or it could be just your voice's warmth
That broods above my body —
Rolling thunder through me.

Lost at sea, each cloud exhales a storm
That trumpets in your honour. Almost
Like your body darkens sweeps of sky,
My thoughts of you hang over me
Like monsoons on the sea.

"Set sail! Set sail inside of her!"
My longing soul bursts out like lightning.
Watching all these brooding swells,
I still set sail a sailor
Always out at sea.

Everydays & Holidays

Blender

He throws bananas in the blender jug.
"You know," he says to her behind him, "there's "A
dating app named 'Blender'." On the rug
She yoga trains, "For gay men?" "What?" he stares.

He stumbles, "I don't really know. The point,"
He presses, while she stretches out of joint,
"So I just wouldn't wanna have to use
A dating app." He pours some mango juice.

She asks, "Why think about the chance at all?"
"Don't be obtuse," he rolls his eyes and sighs.
She stretches backwards, "'Dating app' implies"
"You're stepping out." "It doesn't even fall

"Inside that league... it's... What is this about?"
She sighs, "Just let me finish working out."

Sharpening Knives

She watches while he guides the blade
Across the stone. She says, "That looks bizarre."
He snaps, "I'm in a zone right now," not strayed.
She sneers, her eyebrow raised, "Of course you are."

He rubs his thumb against the knife's edge, glares
And goes ahead. She asks, "How long's this whole
Routine supposed to last?" He stops and tears
Himself away confused, "I'm on a roll."

"What else is there to do?" She scowls, "Let's try"
"Not wasting all our weekend." "Wasting?! How?"
He says, "I have to sharpen knives." Reply
Of death, she stares ahead. He asks, "What now?"

She's silent. "Ugh, okay!" he groans, "You win!"
She smiles, still hushed. He moans, "Whatever then."

A Nice Meal

She chops. She stirs. He watches from the door
And licks his lips. She starts a stove top flame
And takes a shallow skillet. Starts to pour
Some oil. "Mm hmm," he moans. "It's not a game,"

She says, "I need to cook." He comes to play.
And rubs her back, her waist, and leans to try
And kiss her cheek. She grumbles, "Baby, hey!
"I need to cook this food." He rubs her thigh

And asks, "So why does this seem like you need
"To work on something else?" Her cheeks both turn
To shades of blush. He says, "I feel like we'd
"Both like dessert right now." "The food might burn,"

She says. He rubs, "Well, you should make it fast."
She smiles, "You know we always make it last."

Let's Go Somewhere

"Let's go somewhere," she says. He nods his head.
With snow against the window pane, "I guess,"
He says, "Let's just stay home." A look of stress,
She grumbles, sighs, says, "How about, instead,"
"We go do something fun?" A look of dread,
He says, "It's freezing and there's snow." She says,
With wonder, "You still like the ferry, yes?"
He rolls his eyes, "The snow," his arms outspread.

She smiles, "We'll have the ferry all alone."
He laughs, "What good exactly would that be?"
"I mean..." she adds, "Imagine, on our own,"
She says, "like it's our yacht!" she grins with glee.
He shyly laughs, "Of course," beneath a groan.
She hugs him, "Let's go have an odyssey."

Winter Prayers

She lights a candle, cross her heart, and kneels
To pray. He stands aside and looks away
To check his smartphone's time. He leans and steals
A closer look. He rolls his eyes. "Okay,"

She says. He jumps, says, "Huh?" surprised. "Let's go,"
She stands and lets him kiss her cheek. She wraps
Her arms around his waist. He moans too low
For her to hear. He hits the sidewalk gaps

With every step their way back home. She rolls
Her eyes. "You prayed for me?" he asks. "And me
"And us," she says. He answers, "Hmm," and holes
His words up 'til they're home. He turns the key.

Inside, she sees a puppy with *that* cat
Beside. She gasps. He smiles, "You prayed for that?"

Postscript

Fear of Parachutes

"I don't wanna jump!" she screams. "But..." "Why'd
"You bring me up here?!" "Fun." "For who? Not
"Me!" "You're not afraid of heights. I tried
"To think of something both of us would
"Like." She warms a bit, "You're right. I'm not
"Afraid of heights. I don't think I should
"Plummet to my death, though!" "Yeah, I got
"That," he replies. "Well, good," she says, then
Starts to start removing things. But stood
Behind, he latches her to him then
Jumps out. sending them towards the wood
And field beneath them. "Ahhh!" her screams are
Louder even than the wind is when
He pulls the cord, the ground still so far.

End

www.ingramcontent.com/pod-product-compliance
Lightning Source LLC
Chambersburg PA
CBHW032206010726

47493CB00008BA/2857